A CUP of LOVE and Other Short Stories

Surendra Singnar

"Love is life. All, everything that I understand, I understand only because I love. Everything is, everything exists, only because I love. Everything is united by it alone. Love is God, and to die means that I, a particle of love, shall return to the general and eternal source."
--- Leo Tolstoy

BlueRose ONE
Stories Matter
NewDelhi • London

BLUEROSE PUBLISHERS

India | U.K.

For permissions requests or inquiries regarding this publication, please contact:

BLUEROSE PUBLISHERS
www.BlueRoseONE.com
info@bluerosepublishers.com
+91 8882 898 898
+4407342408967

ISBN: 978-93-6783-409-1

Cover Design: Aman Sharma
Typesetting: Pooja Sharma

First Edition: January 2025

DEDICATION

This book, "A CUP OF LOVE," is fondly dedicated to my loving teachers, who shaped me as I am today.

PREFACE

Before publishing this collection of short stories, "A CUP OF LOVE And Other Short Stories," I published ten short stories in different magazines and anthologies, initiated by some genuine and humble publishers in India and abroad. This modern fiction short story book contains seven captivating stories. It covers an extraordinary range of glimpse of another world gone by yet these stories seem timeless, and characters in them show some foibles, fears, and hopes as do people in the brave new world of the present century.

Richly weaved into various strands in life and wrapped in vivacity and spontaneity, these selected short stories of my published works present the readers with varied aspects of my writings. From foregrounding the evils of social crimes to the mysticism and romance of native Indian surroundings, this book stores a casket of experiences and pleasing tales for the readers to explore! Some of the stories entwine the bonding of true love, emotion and heart touching masterpiece in the realm of human life, that everyman encounters. And some horror stories that do more than just send shivers down readers' spines when they read them. They are – A Cup of Love, In the Winter Solstice, At the Mercy of Nature, Writing with Ghost, Lost in Amiss Mate, Dr. Sam and The Big Deals in one family and under the same roof.

This is a work of fiction. The names, characters and incidents portrayed in it are the works of my imagination. Any resemblance to actual persons, living or dead, events or localities, is entirely coincidental.

All the titles of my short stories are like my children whose eyes are just opened and peeped in the world of literature, seeking your good reader's care and love to nurturing them to grow healthy.

With Fond Regards

Author

ACKNOWLEDGEMENTS

While writing this collection of Short Stories, I have more than one occasion remembered the wisdom of the saying – "Thank God we don't get what we deserve in life."

Keeping this wisdom in my heart, I would like to thank all the wonderful people who are being instrumental in bringing out my dream book, "A CUP OF LOVE."

I thank my immediate Publishers – (i) Manoj Kumar Singh, (ii) Jay Chakravarti, (iii) Rajashree Kiran Singh and (iv) ShortsPub (Noida), who have been my inspiration and confidence that ignite my literary urge and its journey to moving ahead.

Last but not least, my intimate publishers, BlueRose Publishers and the team deserve much appreciation for their constant support to bringing out my second book, "A CUP OF LOVE" published by them, which is in your hand with stunning cover design introducing its face to my readers.

Author

CONTENTS

A CUP OF LOVE

Amar has retired from his govt. service recently. Now, he lives with his younger brother, Anand. He loves the fond families of Anand more than himself. Particularly he is more attached with Esika, the lone daughter of the family. One fine morning in November, Amar is relaxing on a wooden relax chair taking the first glow of sunshine on the lawn. He is turning page after page of his old College Souvenir, waiting for his morning cup of tea and his favorite newspaper, The Assam Tribune.

Esika looks fresh in her white top with her sky blue wide leg palazzo pant, coming out with a cup of tea for her uncle, as she does every morning.

"Good morning uncle, why are you gloomy today?"

"No, simply just looking our old College Souvenir," "I think, the hawker is late today for my Newspaper!" Amar wants to divert Esika's attention towards something else…

"Oh, here's your cup of tea, uncle," she says. In the main time, the hawker has stopped his old Hero bicycle, enters the gate, holding some magazines and a copy of The Assam Tribune. Esika goes forward to take the newspaper from the hawker. She notices the current issue of Women's Era.

"Uncle, may I have a copy of Women's Era?" she says.

"Okay, okay, get it," he says. Esika is elated to have the November Issue of her favorite magazine.

"Thank you, uncle, this is your Newspaper," she says. Esika is excited to have a quick look at the contents of the month and some pictures on them. She walks in but her eyes are fixed on the pages of the magazine.

After having seen the headlines on first page of The Assam Tribune, Amar has turned few pages before reading the Editorial, his most loved page of the newspaper. He has noticed a pink color Leaflet between the pages. He picks up the leaflet, and there it reads…

"The Ex-Students of Diphu Govt. College are organizing the Alumni Association Meet on the last Sunday of November. All concerned Ex-Students are cordially invited in the Alumni Meet on Sunday Evening."

Chitra Mukherjee

Convener

Ex-Students' Alumni Association

Leaving all important contents of the newspaper, Amar has concentrated on the Appeal Letter through the pink Leaflet arranged by the local advertising agency. He has seen and heard the name 'Chitra' after thirty years. He reads again and again but can't believe the name, Chitra, the long lost name from his life. But not from his heart, it has been preserved since Chitra parted from his life. Amar is deeply engrossed and plunged into his past life.

Amar met Chitra in Diphu. He was a day scholar at Diphu Govt. College. Chitra was a hosteller of the Girls' Hostel of the College. She hailed from a modest-class Bengali family. She was a brilliant student and good in every field: music, singing and literature also not bad in minor games. Chitra was barely sixteen when she admitted in Pre-University class in the College. Amar was twenty two and in his BA first year. Amar was an average student and was without that fire in the belly to achieve anything outstanding in life.

But Amar was a good human being. His non-imposing personality, laid-back attitude and pleasant demeanor were attributes that Chitra liked about him. Chitra enjoyed hanging out with him during the weekends when they were allowed trips to the nearby Botanical Garden and square. It was an easy friendship between them. They started writing to each other and, before Chitra realized it, Amar became her best friend with whom she could talk to about anything under the sun. She knew that Amar would never rat on her, no matter what.

The last night of boarding for that term was teary-eyed for all of them. They had their personal diaries filled with addresses and phone numbers of the seniors who were leaving college, and they all promised each other to remain friends for the rest of their lives.

During the last one-year studies in Diphu Govt. College, Amar found all moments spent with Chitra were fantastic. Every bit of their meetings was so deeply entwined in his heart and as did Chitra. He remembered how Chitra and her hostel mates waited with their hold-alls and packed bags for their families to collect them. On that day, everyone had gloomy face and amidst teary goodbyes to friends and professors, Chitra left for home after finishing her first year at Diphu Govt. College. How Amar was standing outside the College gate waiting for Chitra to say goodbye.

Chitra asked the driver if he could stop the car. When they stopped, she got out of the car and pressed a note with her house address as well as with the phone numbers into Amar's palm. Chitra told him that they would stay in touch till she returned for the next term. Chitra was happy to go to Lumding, her home-town.

After Amar got acquainted with Chitra, they used to have their cups of tea in every evening at a nearby Bengali Tea

Stall, a stone throw distance from the main gate of the College campus. Chitra called the owner of the Tea Stall *Kaku* - uncle. Chitra was one of those girls studied in Diphu Govt. College whose serene brow, courageous eyes, and well set mouth and chin signified largeness of her mind and dignity of character. She was a girl of great charm and fascination.

Days after days, weeks after weeks and months after months, Amar and Chitra became closer and more intimacy. They began to love each other. Their love affairs had been lasting for years till Chitra passed her BA with honour in Education from Diphu Govt. College and Amar did his MA in History from Gauhati University.

A news came to Amar that Chira was engaged with Dr. Abhijeet Mukherjee, a reputed Surgeon in Kolkata, it was like a bolt from the blue. He failed to understand the reason behind their break-up. He kept on pondering for quite a long time. Finally he remembered what his Tribal friend had told him once.

"Amar Bro, Bengali Brahmin families are very particular, they are well cultured and disciplined. I don't think they will agree to your marriage proposal. Anyway you may try your luck..."

After two weeks, amidst broken-hearted and solitude, a postman delivered a *Wedding Card* to Amar. He had already guessed it's of Chitra's Wedding Card! The Card was found sealed and sent by Regd. Post. Amar was astonished and thought it funny!

He looked around to make sure that no one was within the reach of sight. He'd sat relined on his relax chair and slowly and carefully opened the Card. He found another well folded letter inside the Card. It reads...

"My dear *AMAR*,

I beg apology of you. Please forgive me for my failure to keep my promise. I know the news will hurt you. I've no option but take it as my fate. Be strong as before, face the reality and dare to live… I shall be waiting for you on my Wedding Day. We shall have a cup of tea together as we did at *Kaku*'s Tea Stall!"

Yours *CHITRA*

He boarded in Kolkata bound 15960 Kamrup Express after midnight from Diphu Railway Station. His heart was burning but he took it as his new beginning of life with a hope to have a cup of tea with his lost love, Chitra at her Marriage Party.

Amar lost himself in a maze of thoughts that were rendered vague by his lack of words to express his darling Esika and her mother Aarti, his brother's wife.

"Uncle, what's wrong with you?" Esika says.

"Nothing, just not feeling well, that's all! I'm OK!" Amar says.

"Esika, what happened to Uncle?" Aarti says.

In the main time, booth Esika and Aarti come closer to Amar. They notice the Pink Leaflet that Amar is still holding, leaving his favorite Newspaper aside! Esika has gone through the leaflet and notices the content of it and the name, CHITRA at the bottom. Her eyes give hint her mother. Aarti has understood and pretended as if she knows nothing.

Amar has felt awkward and tries to normalize the atmosphere. He is caught… he thinks. He feels a little bit ashamed of his discreet. He just smiles at them…!

"You know, Aarti, I'm lucky again," Amar says.

"Wow! What's that?" both Aarti and Esika cheer up!

"Relax... I mean, I'm getting another Cup of Tea with my Chitra!" he says.

"How and where!" Esika says.

"I'm meeting Chitra again after many years, here in Diphu," he says.

"Okay, Uncle. Good Luck!" Esika wishes him.

And the day has come. By a strange quirk of fate they have met again several years later. After the Alumni Meet is over, Amar and Chitra have gone down to the same Tea Stall where they had their cup of tea almost in every evening during their College days. This time they find *Kaku* as an old man. His son Arun also has grown up, who is looking after the Tea Stall. *Kaku* has become *Dadu*- grandpa by now. The owner is elated to have Amar and Chitra together again. They touch the feet of the old *Kaku* as they have met after many years.

"Stay blessed! May God bless you," he says.

"I'll make special tea for you with my own hand," he says.

Amar and Chitra sit on the same chairs and at the same table as did they during their heydays. They enjoy their cup of tea: the Tea of Love and quench their longing thirst to their hearts' content. After having their cup of tea, Amar and Chitra take leave of their *Kaku* and they are off.

"What a matching lovely couple they are! May God bless them!" the old *Kaku* says. He thinks that Amar and Chitra are husband and wife. But this isn't, this is just A Cup of Love. What a strange life!

The End

IN THE WINTER SOLSTICE

Nancy had a happy family, living a modest life in an outskirt of a fast growing city in Northeast India. Things were good. Her two children were grown up. Aman was in his 10th standard and Naya was in her 8th standard. Nancy and Aswin were happy at the excellent academic results of their children since they had been sent for schooling. But it was not meant to be. Nancy's husband had been the black sheep in the family which turned into turmoil, full of panic.

Before every Winter Solstice night in every year, Aswin got warning of the consequences in his disturbing dreams: the omen of the dark days to come or something super natural spirit that would loom in his life! The nightmare had happened so real, as if he had seen something strange encounter that had been haunting at a mysterious connection with his past life. He would become restless and irritated for two to three days before the Winter Solstice night to occur in every year. Suddenly, Aswin sprang up from his bed in that night too. He was shocked and scared.

"Nancy, don't hold me, don't hold me up, I must go, I must go, else she would come. Look she is waiting for me ... let me go..." Aswin screamed in his half conscious mind of his energy body.

This strange behavior of Aswin was not new for the family. At least once in a year, Nancy and her two children had to encounter this situation. At the advice of their family doctor, Aswin was taken to a reputed psychiatric doctor in the city. So, it was taken for granted that he would be alright after some years of treatment. But things were not subsided.

It was so coincidence that Aswin made a trip to Shillong after his strange dreams and spent for two to three nights there for the best reason known to him. But he never failed to maintain his yearly routine-trip to Shillong during every Winter Solstice.

No one knew the mystery behind Aswin's past life. Even Nancy for last fourteen years had no idea about his mysterious world he had been living for many years. Only Aswin and Daisy knew the secret of the mystery of their lives. Daisy was a very charming college going girl, the daughter of one of the reputed five star ranking hotel owners in Shillong.

"I was in my deep slumber, last night. You're late. I couldn't even talk to you properly, I am sorry!" Nancy said.

"It's okay darling, I could just manage for the night." Aswin said normally.

"How was your trip to Shillong?" Nancy said. Aswnin was blushed. *'How can she know it?'* Aswin murmured...

"Oh, it's good! My friend took me straight to Shillong from Dibrugarh, that's why late." Aswin said.

"Hope your academic seminar was wonderful!" Nancy said.

"Yes, it was. Marvelous response was there from the crowd, I enjoyed it." Aswin said.

"It's a pride for me that you always come with a surprise." Saying this, Nancy went to the kitchen to get breakfast ready for her loving family. Aswin could simply look at her...

It was after noon. The outside of the house was drizzling. Time to time, gentle winds rustled, the trees around the campus were swaying, a romantic atmosphere prevailed amidst the drizzling rain. Aswin was alone in his reading room. After reading a few pages of his favorite writer, Ruskin Bond's latest book; he became drowsy. In a moment, Aswin's eyes became numb and felt into a deep sleep. He dreamt of a woman being torched alive amidst the crowd. Her painful screams and pleading for help pierced his heart. No one stepped in to help her. The crowded spectators watched her being consumed by the roaring crackling flames. Aswin tried to help her, but he couldn't even move. His legs were chained. He sobbed utterly with pity for the burning woman. He woke up squirming in his relaxing armed chair, and still sobbing.

"What kind of dream was that? What a hell? It was very ghastly, grisly and creepy!" He wondered and was still pondering… The dream he had had kept playing in his mind. He tried to distract himself but it didn't help. He began to decode the strange dream he had dreamt. Finally, his sub-conscious mind had given him a clue to the gruesome murder of his beloved Daisy. Aswin made himself sure that the scene that he had seen in his dream was none but of his beloved Daisy whom he had loved but lost. The screams of the woman in his dream were the calls from his beloved Daisy – the dead but the walking ghost of Shillong.

In Shillong, Ward's Lake is one of the most fascinating sights of tourist attraction. The white colored bridge over the Ward's Lake, the babbling fishes in the lake-water, the cute botanical gardens beside the lake and the most charming and cherishing blossoms of cherry trees lure everyone and relish the minds of all. Amidst the healthy green foliage refreshes one's mind and soul filling with moments of romance. The joy, love and longing all together flourish and dance here in the heart of Shillong. Such love and longing of Daisy for Aswin were the root cause of her dead… and her gipsy spirit still longing for the love of Aswin. She sobbed, cried out and bled from her eyes out of thirst for Aswin's love. Daisy had met Aswin in St. Edmund's College, Shillong and gradually they fell in love. Later, their love lost in the air. Her sister, Nancy had snatched her love from her.

It was again in the Winter Solstice, the darkest night of the year in Shillong. Aswin was restless and became abnormal in his behavior in his hired Cottage Block-E of the Grand Pine Wood Hotel near the famous Ward's Lake. His energy body and wandering spirit had been waiting for his beloved Daisy to appear in the darkest night in Ward's Lake like every Winter Solstice of every year for the last fourteen years in the past. Aswin kept one window half-opened straight towards the Ward's Lake. He had been standing still for hours to appear his beloved walking on the lake-water towards his Cottage, the Block-E.

"Behold! There's she coming ... walking on the lake-water... there're the sounds of her walks on water..." Aswin murmured! There's no light – the street lights and the garden lights around the lake were off due to load-shedding in Shillong even in the darkest night of the year. But, strange! There glowed sharply over the body of an eerie angelic woman in low light. Aswin was shivering with mix-feelings in joy and fright. But, no way, he had to face her else she could harm Aswin. Because Daisy, the ghost wanted Aswin only once in a year in the Winter Solstice night. He looked constantly at the uncanny woman figure walking on the lake-water making splashing sounds on it. Her face was shadowed by her long and thick hair, only her half wrapped bosoms were seen bright and visible. Her slender-waist half clothed with her thinnest white velvet and her long naked hands were slightly visible from the half open window of his hired Cottage. There was the howling of cool winds amidst midnight silence prevailing in the lake. The cool wind

mildly blowing towards Aswin's half open window, where he was standing still like a statue inside.

Whirlpool like winds blew with great force splashing the lake-water on the bank of the lake. Within no time, the winds swirled close to the Cottage, where Aswin was shivering in fright. He immediately closed the half open window and standing at one corner of the room. A radiant figure swooped inside the room through ventilation. Aswin felt a cool breeze through the ventilation, the drapes skimming the walls. With dreamy and blurry eyes, as if within a mist she stood silent. She pushed Aswin at one stroke onto the cozy double bed. Aswin became unconscious and lost his physical body: he was transformed into energy body and deeply mesmerized… and lost in the world of his beloved Daisy – the ghost.

Within his slumber in his vivid dreams, Daisy showed her manifest charm, proven beauty and her thirst for lust… Her white gown was exceedingly transparent, as the full moon's beam revealed, unveiled her heavenly silhouette. She was his lost love: the dead Daisy. Drawing closer her heartbeats got louder, faster, as she had approached, crawled and clawed upon Aswin's bed.

Aswin felt the cozy pressure of her soft bosoms upon him and her scent was mesmerizing, much hypnotic even. His arms held pushed deeply against him; and then the whole of her body engulfed…

She was so cold ghostly even, but the sweetest magical moment Aswin had ever enjoyed. Her lips were like ice pressed upon his. *'My love…'* she mumbled softly. The sweet words left her lips so tenderly… and so passionately; where Aswin was given the most heavenly pleasure with all her best captivating ways.

Daisy, with her deepest pang, she crashed to the ground in agony.

"Look! They echo against within my soul! I must go…" she murmured.

She sobbed again kissing his whole body. She raised Aswin's arms with her long slender hands supporting with her creamy thighs from both sides, and had a passionate last hug.

"I must leave you, now. I've to bid good bye till next Winter Solstice." The ghost said. Aswin said nothing he just didn't want to lose her …

"It will soon be dawn. I'm already late, darling. Let me go, I will return and meet you at the same time here in the next year's Winter Solstice, I promise!" Daisy's body transformed into air and like a white comet she vanished from the place.

This had happened for the third time that chilly week of December during the eve of Christmas. Aswin had been attacked by an unknown fear again, like a worm wriggling through his veins. For Nancy, she couldn't think of celebrating her Christmas this year. The time proved to be a portent of the horror to come. Her stomach was knotted with fear, as if a cold cloud of gloom began to envelop her. She began to drift into a trance. She struggled to remain awake. She heard again Aswin moan in his slightest sleep. Naya, her daughter began to scream out of fear all of a sudden. She sat in a corner burying her face with hands. And then a strange woman was there at the doorstep in her white attire with straight long hair.

Her face was scary with a sallow chilling look, the woman who appeared in Nancy's nightmares. She had taken her to a cold unknown spooky place.

"You made a mistake by captivating my love, Aswin." Nancy was speechless because the strange woman was none but her own sister, Daisy who died many years ago. She couldn't believe herself!

Aswin's agitation grew more and more. She heard him thrashing his limbs and sobbing like a helpless prisoner behind the bar. Nancy wanted to wake him up. But the eerie stare of the strange woman the ghost stopped her from helping him out. The ghost continued to stand at the door.

"Release my love let him go with me as he did in every Winter Solstice in the last fourteen years." The spirit of Daisy said and vanished from the sight. By now, Nancy was sure that the spirit of her dead sister Daisy was disturbing her husband Aswin. She was stunned. Aswin had seen her, too. She was real!

A woman in white, was that the color of her dress? It had been loosely draped. In the dim light, the colors were not perceptible. Everything was dark except her stubborn pale face! Nancy's limbs were getting numb.

"What did she want from me? Did she want more than my Aswin? How can it be possible?" Aswin shrugged his shoulders and lightly pressed his lips. His eyes traversed around in a daze and then he asked a glass of water from Nancy.

"What time is it?"

"Quarter to three."

"I've to be up at seven. I'm going to the office early today for an important meeting. Please don't disturb me till then. Go back to sleep." Nancy nodded and perplexed as Aswin slipped under his coverlet and turned his back to her. She stayed awake and worried till she left the bed at half-past six. She felt exhausted, as if she had run a race for life.

It was a gloomy day, Nancy desperately needed to spend time with someone dearest to her and share her worries with her. Aswin was out of home for his lecture class. She was not in a mood to go to her office. She had applied for three days casual leave. Her children had not yet turned up from their classes. She was lonely in her sitting room; longing to see someone at the moment.

In the profound silence, she began to hear footsteps behind her. She was elated at first, thinking that someone was coming to her. But the steps were different and fishy unlike her shuffling ones. Someone had doggedly started following her. And she wanted her to know. Her legs began to tremble. Her breathing became loud and rapid. She became convinced that she would push her from behind and throw her into the ground. Then she heard a ghostly queer voice, it hit her ears. Her voice struck terror in her racing heart.

"I want nothing from you but my lost love, Aswin. I want your husband once in a year in the Winter Solstice, only for one night." Saying these, the energy body, the unseen ghost was off the scene.

Nancy was terrified. She thought of not detaining her husband, Aswin from going to Shillong and to spend with her dead sister's spirit- the ghost once in a year in the Winter Solstice night. She had resolved to sacrifice her husband for the sake of peace in her family. Aswin was again on his journey to Shillong on 21, December in the pretext of attending a Convocation Programme of North East Hills University. This time, Nancy had no doubt about Aswin's purpose of visiting Shillong. She had made it sure of the Winter Solstice night of the year from the *Panjika*-calendar which fell in the night of 22, December the day in which Nancy's sister Daisy was murdered. She gladly accepted the call of her sister, because she knew that Daisy was killed by an unknown murderer whose identity was untraced and undiscovered. But the continuation of Daisy's captivating had been continuing since Aswin married to Nancy. The mystery was remained unearthed till then.

After the gap of three decades of their married life, Aswin had retired from his service as a senior professor of a reputed college of the city. However, this time he wanted to spend the rest of his life with his first love: the dead Daisy- the living ghost to appease her spirit. Nancy could read his mind... she decided to part with him to fulfill the last wish of her husband for the sake of her dead sister, Daisy.

Aswin, the retired professor had booked the same old cottage but now updated with modern amenities. He was relaxing on the bed and reminiscing his past: the magic moments spent with his lost love – the ghost.

As the sun fell, Aswin waited as he had in every Winter Solstice for the last three decades. His thoughts now hazed upon his mind. His body aged from wear and years of living. His mind scrolled pondering on his memories. The last lust passion of Daisy for him awaited, the soulless beauty of the night... his body ached as he turned to view his half open window. The drapes were blowing within the cold breeze as was their every liaison in the past. She appeared as heavenly angel this time, a unique way of love making approach. Un-aged! Skin unblemished soft as her lips rolled.

Aswin felt her against him, her scent invigorating, what was left of the life within him. Her voice warmed him as she whispered –

"My love, it's time, you'll become immortal like me."

"What may come I'll embrace for your sake!" Aswin said. They embraced within one another's arms. She tenderly kissed him, snarled as she plunged pierces her fangs upon his aged skin. Aswin felt more pleasure than pain, as she drank the purity flew upon her lips. Her ageing body, her spirit life-force was soul returning to her. Warming his body, they laid within one another's embrace.

"This is our last night my sweet baby!" she whispered sweetly upon his ear.

"At dawn our bodies will rest, our souls will entwine ascending to the heavens." The ghost moaned with her deepest sigh!

Then the twin spirits vanished into the air in the Winter Solstice night. Only the dead body of poor Aswin, the lover of Daisy was lying on the floor of the cottage.

***

AT THE MERCY OF NATURE

In 1951: A boy was lost. A boy of nine years old *Sam* was lost in a nearby jungle of a village- *Rongkim*. Panic prevailed everywhere. There was hue and cry among the villagers. The villagers were running to and fro adopting every mean to provide inputs for finding out the lost boy. The gigantic village headman roared like a lion in anger, holding his long handmade gun.

"How can a boy get lost from my village? Whose work is this?" He looked at the helpless crowd.

"My Chief, please do something, get my *Sam* back," *Sam's father* said, "You know I have no second son." The headman had obliged and ordered all his men to search the lost boy combating every nook and corner: the caves, the springs, the rivers, the hills and mountains.

The search operation was intensified rigorously day and night. But alas! No trace of *Sam's* whereabouts was discovered. *Sam's* mother, *Kungri* had been lying unconscious since the day *Sam* had disappeared in the jungle. She could only murmur…

"My child, *Sam*, where have you gone, come back my child… I shouldn't have taken you… it's my fault… I shouldn't have taken you… I shouldn't have taken you…!"

Days, weeks and months passed by, the villagers failed to find out *Sam*. The villagers were tired of searching him. The whole area of the jungles was searched but in vain. *Sam* was not found.

The human efforts collapsed. The only hope of the native for the well being of the lost boy was now bestowed on nature: the mother earth. The whole tribal people of the village surrendered before the unseen spirit – *Hemphu*, the Lord. And finally they washed their hands.

In those days, the mother earth – nature was the provider of all the needs for the livelihood of men abounded abundantly in the forests. The mother earth had provided every need: food, clothes and shelter and their daily needs. For food – yams and sweet potatoes, for vegetables – different kinds of wild edible herbs and plants, bamboo shoots, wild mushroom and for nutrition – varieties of wild edible fruits abound in the jungles. Men lived just at the mercy of nature and protected by the Unseen. Even wild animals too, had their own discipline and principle. Men and animals maintained their coexistence as nature cared them equally.

Several years rolled since *Sam* the son of *Kungri* had lost. Kungri had faith in her unseen gods and deities that wherever might her son be, he was under the care and protection of nature and the deities of jungles. Thus she consoled herself.

"*Neng* (sister-in-law), *munhai* (brother's daughter) is now grown up, I'm afraid, my dream to make her my daughter-in-law will never fulfill!" *Kungri* said to her brother's wife *Kareng*.

"You're right *neng*, *Hanri* is now a girl of sixteen, after few years of wait she will have to go to her own home," *Kareng* said, "But don't worry *neng*, if God wishes miracle may happen at any time."

"No hope *neng*, my dream has already shattered! It remains as a dream only," *Kungri* sobbed.

"Stop weeping *neng*, it's all in the hand of our *Hemphu*: the Lord," *Kareng* said, "Let's go to the *Jhum* (farm), our group is also advancing."

Both *Kungri* and *Kareng* had picked up their baskets and hang on their shoulders and joined the group. The villagers regained their enthusiasm like before as they had been living in the hills for centuries. Notwithstanding, the headman couldn't bear the loss of his prestige. He was under mental depression for not able to find out his village boy the only son of his friend. He felt himself disgraced and worthless!

"Why are you so upset nowadays?" his wife asked.

"You know, I feel weaker mentally since the boy had lost from my village," headman said, "The whole headmen of my neighboring villages regarded me as a highly esteemed headman among them, but I deserve this honor no more now, I feel dejected!"

"Who said so? Who told you this? I don't think so. Still you deserve the same worth and prestige as you were," his wife said.

"But I can't take it easy! I take it as my duty to save every soul living in my village," he said.

"Of course, it is. But one's fate can't be changed," the wife said, "All this depends on one's fate, no one can alter. It was their fate, you can't help them out." She continued, "Now forget all this ill thinking and eat your favorite yam and drink the red tea."

She offered him a bowl of hot red tea to drink with the boiled yam she had collected from their *jhum-farm*. They both felt relaxed and refreshed mentally after drinking the tea. Their pet dog, *Subong* was waiting for the remnant piece of the yam from his master.

After ten years of elapse since the lost boy incident, the headman had a longing for hunting. He hadn't used his double barrel gun for a decade due to his agony and disgrace for he was unable to find out the lost boy, *Sam.* He sat on a wooden mortar under the morning sun and was cleaning the half rusted gun with rugged piece of cloth and animal's fat-oil. In the mean time, an early hunter, *Sikari* came running to the headman holding his gun, as if a wild animal was chasing after him."My chief, my chief, there… there… a human figure is spotted at the stream near a mighty banyan tree in the deep jungle… I have seen with my own eyes…" *Sikari* said. He was nervous. The headman sprang up. At once, he thought of the lost boy, *Sam.*

"When did you see?"

"This early morning, I come straight to you. I could have fired at him but… he seems like human being with long hair. Very strange creature so I didn't fire at him. I was scare!" *Sikari* narrated.

The headman made it sure for Sam. Without saying anything he open fired his gun after ten years. He was cheered up and laughed for the first time after a long silence.

"Come one and come all, bravo! Our gods and deities had heard our prayers, there will be good news soon for us… come one, come all…" the headman shouted at his highest pitch.

Within no time all villagers had gathered at the call of the headman and the sound of his gun. The villagers thronged at the headman's house. They all kept their ears and eyes opened looking at their headman for the surprise tiding.

"Come all the young and strong ones. Let's follow *Sikar*i and move towards the jungle. Today will be our day. Come on…" the headman called upon all to follow him while *Sikari* was in the lead.

The folks gathered in multitude at the headman's house, anxiously waiting for their return. After a long wait, by the evening the group came back. The stronger men fetched a strange creature from the jungle. His body and hands were tied up from his back. He uttered some loud strange sounds of call to somebody, he was missing. The villagers were panic. They all dispersed back out of fear of the creature. The strange human-like creature looked at them in terror. He was a mood to attack the crowd. Of course he was in panic and fear for his life. Some of his childhood friends could recognize him to be *Sam*, the lost boy. They tried to go near to him but they were afraid. The strange creature was unfriendly by now. Many had identified and recognized him to be *Sam*. But no one dared to go closer to him. The headman was sure that the strange creature was none but the lost boy, *Sam*. He was extremely elated, his joy knew no bounds.

Amidst the tensed moment, *Kungri* came running from nowhere jostling the crowd. She had gone closer to the strange creature, stared at him, watched carefully while the panic creature with long hair, long nails with hairy body stood motionless and became emotional. *Kungri*, the mother wept loudly and hugged the strange man.

"O my child, my *Sam*, where you'd been for so many years… why did you leave me alone like this? Please unshackle him he is my *Sam*, my only child!" *Kungri* wept louder, while the strange man had embraced and put his head in the mother's bosom. The mother and her son had recognized each other. The motherly instinct of a woman was so strong that it could calm down the ferocious man, the lost *Sam*.

The huge crowd was amazed and stunned.

"Perhaps Nature: mother earth had fed *Sam* and fostered him for the last ten years! What a selfless love of Nature for Mankind!" The multitude glorified.

***

WRITING WITH GHOST

It was evening with clear skies. Before dusk, the hilly terrain owned pristine scene that enchanted me before stepping into the Bungalow. A well built physique Forester, Bikram of his forties and an old Watchman, Chehetri who was retiring shortly, were waiting for me to welcome. The driver of the Gypsy provided by my Ranger had hardly managed the vehicle to reach my new service station, Socheng Forest Beat as a Forest Beat Officer in an interior place closed to Meghalaya border.

"Good evening and welcome sir," The Forester saluted me and the Watchman followed... I took their greetings and smiled with my utmost enthusiasm.

"Well, hope everything is fine."

"Yes sir, it is..."

Chhetri had opened the door and windows of the bungalow owned by Forest Department. The bungalow was old enough, but it was maintained well.

"Chhetri, it seems you keep the bungalow well!" I looked around the rooms and the surroundings.

"Yes hajur." Chhetri, the watchman was elated.

"Sir, I take leave of you, else I will be late."

"Okay, you may leave now, take care. Don't stop on the way." I gave him some currencies as tip.

"Thank you, sir. Bye..." The driver was off with the roars of his Gypsy.

The first night at the bungalow was like a solace for the weary traveler. My exhaustion due to the tedious journey, I had traversed. I found everything cozy – the bed, the mattress, the blanket and even the hard pillow. My veins became numb, my body exhausted, wanted for rest.

After Chhetri had served us the supper, Bikram and I ate it and I went to retire soon on the bed, perhaps I was the first man to sleep on it after a very long interval. I could smell its dusty smell came out from the bed – the mattress, the pillows and the clothes that I'd used. In spite of all these uncomfortable situations, I fell in my deep slumber for the night.

At the night, perhaps one by one the clock on the wall struck midnight; when the sounds died away the deep silence of the windless night fell again over everything around the bungalow. At the time, I woke up when the clock had stricken three, even my brain wasn't refreshed – I couldn't immediately recall where I was sleeping in the night. It took me a few minutes to recall my memory back. Finally, I was certain about my being at the moment.

My head was still heavy and my eyes were dreamy… I'd wiped my eyes then saw a glass of water on my side table. I took some gulps from the glass and sprinkled on my eyes. When I'd looked at the other room - the drawing room, it seemed the door and the windows were left opened. The breezy air was blowing from outside and the flickering lights of fireflies came into the room. I hardly got down from my bed – my door was also kept opened. I tip-toed into the drawing room, there too, all windows and doors were found opened.

"Why didn't Chhetri close the doors and the windows of the house? Perhaps, he had forgotten…!" I murmured… I didn't know when Bikram and Chhetri had left for their homes. I entered every room and managed to close the doors and windows of the house for it was only 2 O' Clock at night. I had come to my bedroom and fell into a sound and dreamless sleep.

The tinkling sounds of utensils in the kitchen had awoken me from my sleep. I noticed the wall clock it was fifteen minutes to seven in the morning. I got up and went inside the bath room. The moment, I was about to open the door, Chhetri gave a mild knocks on the door with humble voice.

"Hajur… hajur…" I opened the door.

"Sahib, this is your tea," he put a cup of red tea and a piece of loaf on the plate. Chhetri stared at me with hidden questions on his eyes. A bit strange look and eerie, he looked at my eyes but said nothing.

Without making any words, Chhetri left my room. I saw something strange and spooky on his face – and his unusual body language. I could guess something bizarre. Anyway, I had kept quiet for some time and took my tea and the piece of loaf.

I went into the office-cum-reading room, where I had put my writing tools- the planner bulletin, my pens, my pencils, sharpener, eraser, some note books and my half-written manuscript of a Horror Novel all dumped on the writing desk. By this time, Chhetri was busy making breakfast because there was no cook. He was the one who did every household chore and cooked for his officers whosoever posted there in the past

I was busy arranging my goods including few books, stationery items and food stuff lying scattered on the ground. Suddenly I noticed some petals of *Rajnigandha*, the tuberose flower kept on my incomplete Horror Novel. I was astonished! I thought Chhetri had brought them and kept on it as an alternative for an aerosol spray. I kept them aside on the writing desk.

I arranged all my belongings in order. While arranging my eyes caught sight of few books in a small but unique bookshelf. They were dusty and their cover pages were half-faded. Since I am a lover of books and an amateur writer, the old dusty books fascinated me. I took them out and wiped the dusts out of the books with my towel. Completely strange to see a Novel of *Khasi* (a major tribe of Meghalaya state) language, written in Roman script. I had read some sentences and tried to decode, but unable even to guess. I am astonished to find another antique book, *The Mysterious Affair at Styles,* the first book of Agatha Christie published in October 1920. I'd not only guessed but also made certain that once who lived in this bungalow was fond of books and mysteries! I sensed something queer incidence had taken place here in the past. I'm thrilled to adventure more and discover some more mysteries that would certainly help advancing my writing on mysteries.

In the mean time, the creaking sounds of Bikram, the Forester's shoes were heard. He was a local resident of a nearby village.

"Chhetri..., what are you doing?" Bikram stepped inside the house.

"*Hajur, nasta bana rahahu,* making breakfast," he said.

"Okay, well done, Chhetri." Bikram had come straight closer to me.

"Good morning, sir," he greeted me with a sharp salute.

"Very good morning," I looked at him.

"Sir, you had a good sleep last night?"

"Yes, I had a very good slumber… and the weather is like that of Shillong!"

"Yes, sir, but I thought you had problem with your sleep!"

"No, not at all…," holding the last book to clean its dust, I said, "Why?"

"Simply… because it's first night for you in the bungalow," he murmured.

Bikram tried to normalize its intense motive.

"Let's go to the drawing room."

"Okay, sir."

"Sir, *hajur*, breakfast is ready," Chhetri darted.

"Oh! Okay, we'll go to dining room now," Bikram led me to breakfast table.

We were having our breakfast together at dining table. Chhetri was standing behind us like a housewife, ever ready to serve us. At the same time, he was looking around, as if someone would come and join the breakfast.

"Why are you behaving unfamiliar?" I eagerly asked Chhetri.

"Nothing sir, simply," but still his eyes balls moved around…

"By the way, Chhetri, perhaps you had forgotten to close the doors and windows last night!"

"*Kya*, what…!"

"I mean, you forgot to close the doors and windows last night."

"Oh! No. No, sir," his mouth dried up, he couldn't believe his ears.

"I thought, you only had kept all doors and window open early this morning," Chhetri said.

"What! I can't understand."

I was bewildering! I stopped to chew the piece of *roti*, the food in my mouth. I was enigmatic, because I had found all doors and windows open in the night and I closed them with my own hands. "What's Chhetri saying?" Anyway, I suspended all thinking from my mind for time being. But, I was excited to know the hide and seek game. Something strange veiled mysteries haunted the bungalow. Thinking of the petals of *Rajnigandha*! And the open doors and windows!! I was petrified a bit...!

Amidst perplexed situation, we had our breakfast. Bikram and I set out for side patrolling for the first day of my duty. Bikram took me to most of the areas of the Reserved Forest and the path - the boundaries with other adjacent Meghalaya state. I was amazed to see the beautiful forest lands, abounded with pine trees everywhere creating romantic atmosphere in the forests. Living there anyone can fall in love with... It's so enchanting!

"Why didn't most of the Officers posted at the Beat like to stay here?"

"Sir, there's something untold mysterious story behind...!"

"What?"

"Sir, this is untold story! The hidden mysteries!!

We rested a while. We seated on a fallen wood, breathing fresh air to normalize our exhaustion. Bikram gave me his water-bottle to drink.

"But I would like to spend my entire service length here in these pristine hills. Really, they are lovely and blissful!" I lost myself in thought for a while.

"I wish it she is alive, she would enjoy the pine trees and the small brooks to her heart content! She's a lover of nature." I plunged deep into my past…

"Hey sir, it's time to return," Bikram alerted me.

"Oh yes, we've come far distance…"

In return, we came along the zigzag and up and down track in the forests.

The night was winter solstice, the longest night in December. The moon would appear after midnight only. I was tired due to a long walk I'd undertaken on the day with Bikram. But I had a strong urge to write my ongoing Horror Novel this night. Bikram had gone to his old unrepaired Dormitory to retire and Chhetri had gone to his barrack for the night.

The bungalow where I lived had no electricity, just kerosene lamp. The current posts and wires were seen but no current since then due to some unknown reasons in the hills villages. My body needed rest. So, I'd decided to have a short sleep for some time before I could sit at my writing desk to continue writing my book – the Horror Novel. I had not been sitting at my desk for long when the lamp… went out, and something moved very softly and quietly past me in the room… Something cold and icy touched one of my hands and felt its way up towards my neck and throat. It seemed it was behind me then again it was before me. Then it was over me. I was in the arms of the snow-like angel in her bridal costumes. The lightest touched on my body mesmerized me. I was shivering… the chilling moment kept me spooked. Thereafter, I was in another world, the fairy land.

I had a deep slumber in the night. I had an amazing dream last night full of mysteries, fresh and crystal, very lively.

When I woke up, still I was seated on my bed feeling cold. I wrapped my body with a new Burmese furry red blanket of double size. I felt warmth and cozy on my bed, bending my legs inside the blanket. I'd just closed my eyes and recalling the last night's dream.

"I don't believe in ghosts or spirits. Of course I enjoy ghost scary dreams," I said to myself. This time, too I'd enjoyed the ghost dream. While recalling the eerie moments in the dream, I fully concentrated deep in my conscience time and again to recall them completely live. I was at the state of my subconscious mind… and all the scenes were floating in front of my inner eyes exactly what I had dreamed in the night.

The ghost in my dream talked to me and it was she – my bride, *Riazina* whom I lovingly called *"Rajni."* Her death after our marriage engagement was mysterious. She was from Catholic family background and I am from an Animist family. Our engagement was mutually agreed upon from both families. My in-laws had less of objections than that of my families. However, my mom and particularly my dad were overjoyed to have my engagement with an enlightened Christian tribal family from Meghalaya. Finally our Engagement was solemnized in the main Cathedral of Shillong. On the third day after our engagement, I received the sad news – Riazina my sweetheart Rajni was no more. I was completely numb and broken. My cherished dream was shattered. The dreams of my mom and dad were unfulfilled.

The actual cause of the death of my beloved Riazina was kept top secret. I could sense. Yet, I knew no clue to my bride's death. I could do nothing, but only regrets and agony loomed over me. Since then I couldn't think of marrying another girl.

I tried to forget the jolt I'd received in my past life. But her sincere discloser about her boyfriend before our engagement tormented me all the time. I remembered what Riazina told me once when we're in the Semester in College in Shillong about her boyfriend, who one-sidedly loved her beyond measure. His love was an unrequited one. I insisted her to tell the name of the boy. But she had never pronounced his name. She begged me to not even think of him. So as I did swear.

Inside the blanket, the hair of my entire body sprang up, and my skins were moving around.

"Raj, I know you couldn't forget me, because our love was pure and true," she wanted to touch me but she couldn't... I too, tried hard to go closer to her, but in vain. I could see her in a fairy form a similar face to my bride, Riazina. She lamented, and wept bitterly. I too, cried mournfully.

"Don't cry Raj, We'll meet in Heaven. I'll wait for you at the threshold of my abode," she continued...

"You don't know Raj that I was murdered. Just after midnight, when I was asleep in my room I was stabbed a dozen times and my door was locked from the outside and then the killer fled away," her voice was so murmuring but heard clearly. And it was the voice of Rajni, my darling...

"Before I breathed my last, I'd tried to see his face but couldn't. He came in disguise. But don't worry I'll give you a clue to him one day...and give me justice!" And then she vanished from my sight.

By then, I'd regained my consciousness and could feel everything normal. But my body was still sweating and shivering. My lung heaved up. My tears were still hot and rolling down from my cheeks. I sat on my bed for a quite long time. I recollected the whole episode.

After my fresh up in the morning, I sat at my writing desk. The tuberose flower was still lying on my Planner Note Book which produced aroma in the cute reading room. I'd glanced at it and thought of my Rajni my lost love. I changed the name of the main character as Rajni in place of Damini in my Novel. And I got the inputs for my entire Book, **'Writing with Ghost'**. A mild knock was heard at the door.

"Sahib, your breakfast is ready," Chhetri called me for breakfast.

"Chhetri, *andar aa jao*, come inside."

"Hajur…?" He stood in his attention position.

"Is there any flower garden nearby?"

"No, Sahib there's no flower garden around."

"Oh!.."

"Why sir? Do you want flowers?" he continued…

"I can get them from my sister's house, she lives in Meghalaya border."

"No, I don't need. You've already given this." I'd picked up the tuberose flower and shown to him.

"No sir, I haven't …!"

"Sir, *hajur yeh kahan se laaya?* Where did you bring it from?"

"It's okay, no matter. Perhaps, Forester sahib brought it for me!"

Chhetri was perplexed and frightened.

"Let's go. Give me my breakfast." I normalized his complexity. But I had smelt blood. There's something strange going on. I could guess that this bungalow was a haunted house. The tuberose flower, the open doors and the open windows!!! All these were mysteries! Yet I was elated because the storyline of my Horror Novel seemed to be same to same what's happening so often. I was excruciatingly thrilled!

After the elapse of fifteen days, I sat at the writing desk engrossing deeply in my writings. The night was of pitch darkness. I'd been writing since 9 O'clock. It's going to be 12 O'clock by my watch. Still I had full spirit of writing, my passion for writing multiplied and thus my pen was bleeding spontaneously throughout the night. I love scary, spooky stories of spectral phantoms. While a part from the scientific truth contradicting the existence of ghosts, I'd genuinely sensed a supernatural presence in the air. I'd been hearing noises on the ceiling at the same time in the wood and surrounding the house each night. But I scared not, because I'm a ghost story writer for quite a long time. Instead I'd enjoyed every scary moment at night which helped me writing my Horror Novel at present.

In this night too, when the surrounding was soundless, trees were in their deep asleep; another strange thing happened to me. A ghost whispered and groaned, caused things to move and trees to fall. A shadowy figure rushed through the door and the window where I was sitting and writing my unfinished book. To fulfill my eagerness to witness the real ghosts, I'd slowly opened my window slightly without making any sound. I peeped silently towards the ghosts through the window. Somehow, I saw a ghost. It had a skeletal body, surrounded by a white, blurry aura! The figure hovered and didn't seem to have a face. Though I wasn't totally scared but my hairs sprang up and skins rapidly moved around.

It seemed the ghost was moving slowly towards my half opened window. Finally I panicked and shut the window carefully so that the ghost couldn't notice me. The wheezing sounds came nearer and closer to my window. The window hook was out of order. In the main time, I'd tied up the handle of the window with the iron bar on the window with my new towel from inside.

After a while two gentle knocks hit the window. I made it certain that it was the work of the ghost. Thereafter mild air had been passed through the cracked holes of the window. The ghost whispered…

"Don't be frightened, I'm your love Riazina, your Rajni." I kept quiet. I simply listened to her without breaths.

"Thank you, Raj for featuring my name, "Rajni" in your book. I know you care me very much. You know, I brought you the petals of Rajnigandhi to remind you that I'm around you." She wept… It's almost dawn, with a strange sibilant sound, she, the ghost, my Rajni disappeared in the dark jungle. I was moved emotionally and at the same time shivering. I could hardly control myself.

I'd spent a sleepless night at the last night. I could sleep only in the morning, so I was late for everything in the morning. I woke up after 10 O'clock. Bikram, the Forester was waiting for me to take me his home for breakfast, where his wife had been waiting for us in a nearby village.

As I'd rushed in the sitting room, Bikram greeted me with a salute.

"Good morning sir."

"Welcome, very good morning." Chhetri came in …

"Sahib, I didn't make breakfast this morning."

"It's okay, but why? Forester sahib also here, I can share with him." Chhetri was speechless. He simply stared helplessly at the eyes of Bikram.

"Sir, it's me to stop Chhetri not to make breakfast for you. My wife has cooked something as breakfast for you this morning."

"It's my pleasure. I'm lucky today."

On seeing my weary face, Bikram wanted to say something…

"Well, I spent a sleepless night last night. I was disturbed…!"

"Disturbed? Who dared to disturb you at night?"

"Chhetri, didn't you know who had come and disturbed our officer?" Bikram continued.

"No, Sir."

"Actually it wasn't the matter. The fact was that I'd encountered with a ghost last night when I was writing my book."

"Ghosts?" The eyes and ears of Bikram and Chhetri looked wider and silent for a while.

"Yes, a ghost, a known ghost. Not stranger."

"Sorry, I'm afraid I don't follow you," Bikram said.

"Sir, we don't understand," Chhetri added.

"I know, you people haven't told me about this haunted bungalow. But no matter, I've enjoyed being with the ghost last night," I smiled at them.

"Oh No…!" Both Bikram and Chhetri sighed.

"We're sorry sir, in fact we thought that you'll scare and leave us like the other Beat Officers who came and gone within few weeks or months."

"Extremely sorry sir for not telling you the existence of ghosts here in advance, moreover, some people don't believe in ghosts."

"But you know, I'm happy to be here with the ghost." I stood, went near the open window and gazing dreamily into space.

"I'll not go soon from this bungalow, because I long for peace and solitude in life and I've found solace and tranquility here with the ghost – my own ghost, my lost love – my Rajni." I turned to Bikram and Chhetri, holding their arms and with tears in my eyes...

"I promise I'll not go soon from here; I'll be with you for good. I've promises to keep, I've to finish my Novel the vary story of my Rajni: the ghost!

***

LOST IN AMISS MATE

Raj was on his way to the Assam University Campus, Diphu to reach at 10:10 O'clock sharp for his lecture class. He was a new Assistant Professor of History Department, one of the punctual faculty members of the University. His auto rickshaw was at a moderate speed for it was moving through the town. A fast growing town a mini centre of education hub for those aspirants who thronged for their higher education from every nook and corner of the hilly province.

An auto rickshaw from the same direction suddenly had overtaken with faster speed and parked at aside of the main road. It was only five meters ahead of the auto rickshaw, in which Raj was a passenger. A spinster got down hurriedly signaled the auto to stop. Raj was confused thinking about something untoward incidence had happened! He was surprised to see an unknown figure, skinny, lean and thin tall girl approaching him. He couldn't recognize her at his first sight.

The girl had come closer to Raj with a familiar smile as if they're known each other for decades. His legs automatically stepped down the pitched and kept aside on the footpath. She stretched her hand for an intimate hand shake.

"Good morning Raj."

"Very good morning"

Raj was astonished, staring at her from head to toes for few seconds. He couldn't recollect his memory instant. She guessed his clumsy situation.

"Raj, I was your best friend in the school," "I'm Radha"

"Oh, the one who got distinction in School Exams?" "What a surprise!"

"Yes Raj, I'm she. Once I joined in your family trip to Goa" "It was a wonderful trip!"

"Yah yah, it was… it was…" "By the way, I'm in a hurry to my lecture class, see you…"

"Raj, your number, - please…"

He'd read his mobile number and she quickly saved in her mobile.

"See you soon Raj, bye…" She got into her auto, waved her hand and was off.

"Bye…" he waved back in return.

Raj was late by 10 minutes for duty on that day. He's annoyed.

It was late at night. Raj couldn't go to bed on certain reasons: He had to complete his personal works as well as official and the craziness disturbed him most was the strange encounter with the skinny bonny tall girl, Radha, his school mate.

"She is completely a changed girl! Her meekness, soberness all have been vanished from her. She behaves strange and extremely hyper-active. Her way of talking, her body language and pose are completely different from the way she had behaved in her school days. She was one of the most obedient students in the class. Raj remembered how much she'd labored for her success in her matriculation. Finally she got the fruit of her labor: she got distinction with five letter-marks. She brought laurel to the school." - These contrast thoughts disturbed him a lot.

Radha was married to a Contractor's son, Baadal. After few months of their marriage, Baadal died in a mysterious death. Postmortem report revealed that he died after taking overdose drug. Since then, she had been absconding from her parents as well as her in-laws, too. She lived a life of vagabond.

"Now, Radha is a super smart and ultra-modern girl in this colorful town." - But strange!

"Strange really strange how girls are adaptable with the winds of change in the varied societies."

Various unending thoughts perplexed his mind after meeting Radha. In fact, she was his most adorable girl in his class for her sincerity, endurance and simplicity in nature, she'd possessed. She was an introvert.

In a cold winter night, fifteen past eleven was like more than midnight. Raj used to keep his cell phone switched on even at night for he needed to hear every bit of information about his ailing mother who was far away from his place of work. He was almost asleep at that night. Unexpectedly a phone call came in. His heart shrank! Good God! It wasn't a call from home. He relaxed. It was an unknown number.

"Raj, it's me - Radha. Sorry for my untimely call!"

"Oh! Radha? It's okay. What can I help you?" It's a natural response from everyone.

"If you don't mind, I need your help *dost* – my dear friend."

"Never mind…" came from his mouth.

It was quiet for a moment.

"Yes, Radha what's your problem? Are you alright?"

"I'm not alright *dost.* I'm threatened!"

"What? You're threatened?"

"Yes *dost*!!" Her voice was shaking…

Taking it as granted, he was excruciatingly perplexed! Radha was still sobbing…! He guessed.

"Hello, hello…"

"Yes Raj, sorry *dost*, extremely sorry!" Her sobbing sound was heard louder.

"It's okay. Tell me exactly what had happened to you." Raj deeply absorbed in her matter.

"Well, it's already midnight. See me tomorrow morning. Good night."

"Okay *dost*, good night."

Raj was distracted by Radha's phone call. His heart ached much, for Radha was very well known to him. And he loved her most among his class mates. He couldn't sleep straight away that night. Besides, Radha was quite untraced for him for several years. It was almost twelve years after the School Convocation, where they're applauded amid the crowd parents and guests packed in the school hall: the cheered and shared moments of their victory and joy.

Raj wasn't sure for her to come because she didn't know his place of stay here in this mini but very complex town. Roads are multiples and numerously crossed roads. He woke up considerably late in that morning. Raj was very fond of personal care. His white softy towel on his shoulder, his new pact of Sensodyne tooth paste and brush were in his left hand and with right hand opening the new pact of his morning friends ever. He enjoyed taking shower every morning for he'd missed all these modern amenities in his young golden days. While taking shower, he forgot about his day's schedule and engagement. Appointment with

Radha was totally out of his mind. He was ease and in his own world in a pretty marveled bathroom.

Raj has a habit of checking his phone while he's free from his morning duties and domestic cores. In that morning, too, he didn't have a look at his Samsung android phone even. After taking his lukewarm showers, Raj sat on his bed. He looked fresh and enthusiastic. Stretching out his left hand he put his fingers under his white spongy pillow. He looked at closed on the screen of his phone.

"Oh my God, lots of missed calls," he checked out all. He found there were twelve missed calls from an unknown number. Raj thought of calling back this call first.

"Hello, May I know whose number is this?" he softly spoke.

"Oh No! I thought you've saved my number'" "It's me – Radha, your blue eyed girl."

"Sorry, I forgot to save it, sorry *yaar*! - My friend..."

"It's okay Raj, my friend. But next time no excuse."

"Okay, okay, I'll save now."

"I've been waiting for your response, ready to meet you soon." "Location, please – "

"Hire an auto I'll guide him the exact location of my stay." "Will it be done?"

"Yes, I'm off now…"

The auto driver hadn't made any mistakes to drop Radha at the doorstep. It was Sunday morning. Office goers were busy with their family helping domestic chores. Some spared time for outing and picnic spending their leisure times with children they loved. Raj wasn't fortunate enough to enjoy such an occasion because his family stayed in the village. His loving wife, Anjana took care of his ailing mother and his loving child at home. His anticipation for Radha's visit was at hand at the right time. The stopping sound of an auto-rickshaw was heard louder at a point, it stopped in front of the gate. Raj stretched the light pinky window's curtains and peeped.

A moderately tall slim lady in her white attire, *Kurta Payama* -Indian dress got down of the auto, stepped forwards and opened the gate gently. Her excitement of meeting Raj could guess by the movement of her body while walking.

Raj went forward to receive Radha to his rented house a bit outskirt of the main township.

"Hi Radha, good morning and welcome to my hut," said Raj stretching his hands.

"Very good morning Raj, thank you,"

"How are you doing?"

"I'm fine, thank you."

Raj, being a married person, he found himself awkward of the situation. He actually didn't want Radha to meet him like this. He got a bit excruciating!

"Raj, are you okay?"

"Yes, yes I'm fine. Take the glass, it is plain water."

"Thank you, so health conscious! It's good."

Raj occupied a seat opposite to Radha's seat. The glass top of the centre table was dazzling due to morning sunray passing through the open window.

"Raj, come and sit by my side. It seems the sunlight inconvenienced you."

"No, not at all, I'm comfortable here."

"What do you prefer, tea or coffee?"

"I prefer tea to coffee in the morning."

"Okay, done."

Raj went inside the kitchen. Radha moved her head around and looked the well-maintained sitting room. She was impressed.

"Oh, I could have made the tea, why take the trouble?"

"No, no, it's okay. You're my guest this morning."

"Thank you," said Radha and looked at Raj, her bosom school mate. She adored much!

After two to three sips of their tea…

"Now, tell me your problem", said Raj – "There's no one except the full walls of the room."

Radha was hushed! Chilled! She tried to be basic herself. But Raj could easily read her face. She was embarrassed. The memories of her school days flashed back. She recollected all the memorable events - the small incidents befell in those younger days: the sweetest moments. She absorbed herself too deep that she'd forgotten everything. She became retrograde. Her preplanned fraudulence to extract money from Raj was in vain. She couldn't gather courage to misrepresent her ideas to him for money. She mumbled… she came to her present state of mind – the frisky mind.

"Actually Raj, to tell you the fact – I'm a sinner." Radha buried her face with her skinny hands.

"Radha, it's not fair talking like this," Raj said. He tried to console her.

"No, *dost*, I've no right to live on… I shouldn't be alive any more… any more…" she sobbed bitterly. The sitting room abruptly turned into wretchedness!

Raj couldn't refuse since she had been his best classmate. Moreover, they had met each other after fifteen years. Raj thought Radha might have been facing personal problem. If he could help her in her distress, it'd certainly be a great help for her and he'd feel great and proud to help his old teenage friend. He took it as a privilege to help his old classmate in her trouble time. Both boarded in an auto rickshaw where Radha led Raj to her dwelling place. The main gate of the house boundary was recklessly closed, carelessly mended. The room where Radha lived seemed to be negligible. The door of the room was loosely shut. Even a small boy of his go around would easily open and have an access of the room.

Radha had opened the door, the way she opened every time as usual. I thought somebody was inside the room or nearby. Seeing the way the door and the main entrance gate were closed recklessly.

"Come Raj, this is my cottage. I've come to stay here for few months." Radha said showing the next room attached to her.

"This is my friend's room." "We share one kitchen, we eat together."

I noticed the room minutely where her friend supposed to live. I noticed that the room was so neatly maintained and properly arranged although the house and its rooms as well are so ordinarily left to exist.

"Who is your friend?"

"She is Alice. She has gone to her Aunt's house to bring one month's ration. It's not so far from the town."

"I see, how do you get yours?"

"We eat together, and she doesn't mind."

"You're lucky to have such a wonderful friend in these days." "I think she's also hailed from your place?"

"No, Alice isn't from my place. She is from *Nilip* - the northern province of the district."

"It's all right, now tell me what can I help you," "What's your problem?" Raj insisted empathetically.

"Raj, you've to save me, you've to save my life." Radha became emotional.

"What do you say," astonished Raj. "I don't quite understand!"

"I've been absconding myself from their reach. They wanted to kill me!" She shivered.

Radha was abruptly scary.

Raj, since a long time came close to her, and for the moment he was the only closest man in her life – she put her head under the arm of her far-forgotten mate leaving everything aside. She wept. Raj was astonished. He couldn't understand what's wrong with Radha. He couldn't gather much courage to ask her any details.

"Well, now calm down, I'm with you. What's the actual problem right now?"

Radha was still weeping. Her warm tear-drops fallen on his hands. His heart softened. He felt as if his own biological sister cuddled on his arms. Raj's heart was filled with compassion. He decided of helping her out with his most capable ways and means.

"*Dost,* I'm badly in need of money," "I've approached to all the high-ups of the Council," "Told them my problem in length, but no one has paid heed to my plea," Radha lamented. "I'm helpless."

Raj shocked a little bit… he did have extra pockets to help someone. He had a two thousand note in his valet right then. He saved the amount for unseen expenses. He was silent for awhile.

"What happened *dost*?" "You look up set!" said Radha staring his face in a bent neck.

"No, nothing, I'm just lost in our memories." He embarrassed.

"Lost in memory? What memory *dost*?"

"I'm thinking of our school days, how innocent we were then…" Raj pretended!

"Oh, I was then so ignorant and aloofness, you knew my shyness was one of the reasons for my aloofness." Radha regretted!

"Well, Radha keep it with you, more next time…"

"Thank you *dost*, it's so kind of you." She quickly took the note from Raj as if the note was the life saver of the moment.

Radha hugged Raj. He got an intimate hug from a girl for the first time other than his wife in his life. He felt something unusual moment but it was the truth.

"Now, let me go. Take care…"

"By the by, what are you doing at present?"

"Sorry, *dost*. It's of no use for you to know."

"Why do you say so…?"

"I've my own profession that I can't tell you. Forget it *dost*!" Radha was sad.

"Okay, may be next time - next meeting." Raj hastened to his next destination.

Radha also came out of her room to see off Raj. "Bye bye, see you soon", she bid him with her sweetest smile like she did in the school days. As soon as Raj was out of her sight, she swiftly entered her room. She groped for her old Nokia keypad cell phone. She used this phone only for calling to few discreet numbers. She kept it secret. She seldom shared it. She pressed on ten different keys.

"Hello, *Ali Bhai*, I need the *maal* – her dose right now," Radha said hurriedly.

"*Maal* – it's out of stock." "Your number black listed."

"Why? It's a matter of a pinky note only?"

"My boss said to clear the old balance… else I can't help you out this time." "Over…"

"No, no, no listen to me…come and collect it. I want mine – the *aaslee* – origin one."

"Come to my place right now."

"No, I can't go up to your place this day light."

"Okay then, at the same point, in the same style," "I'll pick it up myself."

Since Raj missed out his university history class on that day, he reached the university campus ahead of the scheduled time for his lecture class. He had thirty minutes extra time before the commencement of a lecture in the class.

Before entering in the lecture hall, he seated at a corner of the Teacher's Common Room, looked out his laptop from his bag and seemed busy searching for something important on history subject. His eyes ball roamed around within the reach of the university campus. Students and faculty members were busy, hurrying to their lecture halls; meeting and consulting among students and with teachers of their favorites. Suddenly his eyes caught sight of a tribal girl as if he saw her somewhere at a glance. He looked at her following constantly from the common room. But he confused and was not sure whether she was the one whom he had seen somewhere which he now could not recollect it.

In the lecture hall, Raj could not concentrate in his lecture. His tainted memory of the girl-student disturbed him unceasingly. He passed the lecture period somehow diffused. The lecture was dispersed. Raj came out of the lecture hall. He was still in his stigma in search of the girl he noticed for a while in the morning among the busy crowd in the campus.

Raj was restless. He longed to see the girl once more. Perhaps he'd recollect his memory and identify her for a better cause. He did not want to leave the university campus. His prickled mind entranced him. He'd surely see the girl again. He searched for her at every nook and corner of the campus. One way he was upset and reluctantly had to give up. His feet had already led him walk towards the main road to catch the university bus leading to the main town for his homeward journey.

To his utter surprise, Raj saw the same girl sitting at the window corner of the bus. He looked at her. She could sense his constant sight on her. She got embarrassed. She withdrew her eyes completely from Raj. He could not resist himself from approaching her. He gathered courage to go closer to her. She ignored so that the situation would be developed. She looked outside of the window constantly as if she had more important things to observe.

As the bus accelerated speed, slowly he stood up and approached the girl. She was deliberate of not noticing Raj. He was closer to her.

"Excuse me *bhanti* (sister)," he said "May I know where you are from?"

No response.

"*Bhanti*, I am talking to you," Raj said gently.

"Oh, hi… sorry, I was just… thinking something, I could not make out?"

"May I know where you are from?"

"I am from *Nilip*."

"If you don't mind, may I have your number please?"

"I don't use cell phone!"

"Oh, sorry *bhanti*, I'll obviously see you personally."

The girl said nothing but pretended to be lost in her own world.

In the meantime the bus had geared up at its full speed leaving the big university campus far behind. There was complete silence inside the bus. Only the flapping sounds curtains caused by the outside air were heard. Raj was disappointed and felt dejected. He slowly came to his seat and seated exasperatedly.

The bus went on till its final destination… At a point the bus made "*phhsst*" sound. The bus stopped gently so that no one jerked. Every passenger-student got down one by one. Those who were from a bit outskirt of the main town hired auto-rickshaw for their homeward…

Raj was the last passenger to get down of the bus. He looked at the girl from a close-range and made sure that this was the girl who he saw a framed photograph on the study table of Radha's friend, Alice. Raj unveiled his confusion and made it eminent.

One fine morning at fast peep of cold, Diphu a small but fast developing town was misty and cold. The nature around and the scanty thinly available trees looked gloomy and everything looked hazy. The laborious working class old people, *thella* (pulling-cart) pullers and children shivered in cold. They gathered straw from the nearby paddy field and made fires at different street corners to warm themselves in the heat. By and large, people didn't feel like leaving the bed early. Amidst the foggy weather, Raj walked down to the place where his school mate Radha lived with her friend, Alice – the boarding dormitory.

Raj made a general artificial coughing sound (clearing throat) as a signal of his presence at the door step. No calling bell provision in the dormitory. He knocked at the door. No response came from inside. Raj waited for awhile. He looked around and again knocked at the door pausing a longer seconds. He waited again. No answer came from inside. He looked at his wrist watch it was about eight o'clock. He looked at the surroundings of the house and finally he tried to peep through the wrecked window and lastly knocked the door harder with a pressure with his hand. The door was opened easily. It was just kept shut simply. Raj peeped inside the room and called –

"Radha, are you there?" It was quiet inside. Raj proceeded farther inside the room.

"Hello, Radha are you there?" he called and slowly approached to her room. Radha was still in her deep slumber. She was under her two-layer thick blanket. She managed to bring it from her in-laws. Raj reluctantly woke her up. Radha sprang up from her sleep and hurried hiding her old model small key-pad Nokia hand set under her pillow. She didn't want anybody to know that she had possessed another phone. She used it to call very limited persons for very special purpose.

In a shaky body, she stood up from her bed. She rubbed her eyes, rapped her body with her only night partner – the double-layer thick blanket.

"What a surprise! Raj," she said in her dreamy eyes.

"You're so good that you've come to meet me," she continued, likely to hug Raj.

Raj moved a step backward and skipped.

"To be honest, I've not come to meet you but your friend," said Raj lovingly.

Radha kept quiet for a while. She was disgusted. She thought she was dejected and ignored. She became emotional so casually. She was mentally weak. Her light body was so unsteady. Raj could read her face.

"Do you think I can meet someone else without meeting you?"

"You've not changed much of your jolly way of speaking, I become made of you."

"I like it, I like your style so also love it," she said relaxing her body by stretching her hands.

"Sit *dost,* sit down here on my bed," Radha insisted Raj to sit by her side. Raj sat at a corner edge of her bed.

"My friend, Alice will come at 10 O'clock. She went out early in the morning. She has tuition class for children of the high-ups of the Autonomous Council.

"Oh, I see, your friend is laborious."

"Yeah, she is. After all Alice is from a Christian background."

"Of course, they're particular …"

In the meantime Radha arranged her bed cover properly, folded her blanket. Raj wanted to go out. The morning sunrays had peeped brighter.

"Radha, I'll be waiting outside till your friend comes,"

"No Raj, don't go outside, I don't want you to ..."

Radha wanted him to remain inside the room. She perplexed! Raj guessed. He stared at her.

"Okay, but why?"

"But me not buts," she became dominant.

"I'll make red tea for you."

She entered her small dusky kitchen. The kitchen was old but the housekeeping inside was proper. Raj thought it might be the artistic works of Alice! He was queered, curious: waiting in a blank –

After a few minutes, Radha came with two cups of red tea and two pieces of dried cake for Raj and herself. She put the tray on her bed, the horrible flavor of the red tea oozing its vapors with no aroma of tea at all.

"Take it, I've forgotten how to make tea properly," she said "How foolish I'm."

"It is okay, what matters is your heart."

"Well said, but you know Raj, I'm afraid of them! They will come tonight again!!"

Raj said nothing. He watched her behavior, body language and her emotion.

"Please do something Raj, please *dost* ... my life is bleak."

Raj sipped the tea in delight. He didn't want to make Radha upset. He watched, observed and was surprised! He discovered Radha's secret. "She is no more a normal girl," he murmured. Raj was thoughtful.

Meanwhile, Alice came inside as usual without making any sound. She was meek, mild and introvert. She tiptoed inside her room without any concern for who were sitting or talking. After awhile, Radha called Alice with an intention to introduce Raj to her. Reluctantly, Alice came out of her room to say – Hi

On seeing the guest, she excruciatingly blushed! She thought the man was crazy for her. She'd already met him on the bus. She was perplexed! "He might be a ridiculous, a deranged person. But when she looked at his eyes – she sensed a much more tale to read from him …

"I guess you've something to say," Alice said after her sharp glance at Raj.

He impeded. He was encumbered by Radha's presence. He hesitated talking to Alice. His eyes glanced at Radha's eyes for a moment.

"If you don't mind, I've a personal …" Raj couldn't complete his words where Radha said,

"Never mind, by the by I've to go the bathroom." She picked up her tooth brush and the popular *Colgate* paste and a soap case. She hanged a towel on her shoulder and off to her rugged bathroom – thirty meters away from the dormitory.

Raj withdrew his eyes from Radha, he moved his face towards Alice and looked at her apprehensively. In the meantime, Alice dragged an old crocked *mura* (a stool made of cane and bamboo). She seated at another corner of Radha's bed.

Raj was cool and polite in his approach.

"I hope, you won't take my visit otherwise."

"No, never, by the by I'm sorry for that day's incident!"

"I take it as privilege," he said. "Actually Radha's condition has drawn me closer to you."

"Yeah, I feel bad for her."

"In fact what's wrong with Radha?" he said. "I found her behavior depicted fishy!"

"If I'm not wrong, she is psychotic?" he continued.

"Her mental stage is not sound," she said. "Radha being my friend, I can't tell this to anyone."

"We've to do something for her," Raj said. "Else her condition will be irremediable."

"I'm afraid! She may turn as an itinerant girl one day!!"

Raj was pensive. "Of course, we've to do something for her before long."

"Please …" Alice entreated Raj.

Raj became thoughtful, engrossed deeply for finding solution for Radha's unstable mental state.

"Before we do something, we should meet her parents for their consent," he said.

"That's a wise idea," said Alice. "I'll make a program on this."

"Yes, most definitely," Raj said. "Will she agree on this?"

"Leave that part on me." She said. "The rest is yours."

"Okay, done!" he said. "Genuinely what had happened to her?"

"Better not to talk in length about her right now," she said. "She may create problem!"

"Oh, yes… yes…"

Radha came up from her bathroom and hurriedly came inside. She looked fresh.

It was foggy morning again. Raj and Alice, as acceded, rushed to the Bus Station with Radha. They had a plan and pretext to visit Radha's home in the western part of the district. As it was a pre-plan program Raj had bought three tickets in advance for them in the last evening.

They boarded on the morning. After some minutes, the bus driver climbed up. He occupied his comfort seat, started the bus and held the steering in normal mood. The bus took off. Raj delighted because this was his first journey to westward. By then, there was hue and cry among the bus conductors. They shouted – in their own style to draw attention to the morning passengers towards their buses. They needed more passengers to be boarded. The driver had moved the gear, pressed the accelerator for picking up a smooth move-start of his day's journey. It was pleasant.

To give a surprise, they didn't inform Radha's parents about their visit. The bus stopped at the right stoppage. Radha, Alice and Raj got down from the bus. Radha counted the numbers of their bags. Raj searched for his handy bag, where he carried his laptop, note book and pen. He didn't find it. He looked around, prompted to search inside the bus. The conducted hinted him pointing at Radha. She had picked up all bags. The bags were light. Radha headed Alice, walked up to a few yards farther. Raj followed them through the village dusty road. He didn't have any idea about the distance… how long he had to follow Radha to reach her home. After walking for certain distance, Raj had looked his wrist watch. They had walked for twenty minutes. Raj presumed they had walked for more than one kilometer.

"How long we've to walk?"

"Until we reach home..."

"No problem, we'll stay back and spend the night in this lovely village."

"It will be my pleasure," Radha said.

After walking another more hundred meters, Radha stopped at a point near a green colored wooden gate: welcoming them.

Radha's parents were surprised! They looked at Radha and her two friends at the door step. They guessed Radha brought her friends to this new place for seasonal festive visit for their pleasure winter trip to west. They couldn't say anything but welcomed them to their home.

"Welcome to our poor hut," said Radha's mother.

Sonaram, Radha's father said nothing. He dressed in Indian *kurta* and *payama* well matched for his tall and slim physique. He stayed at home. His school got a local holiday. He was busy with his school work, evaluating answer scripts of his students in the sun under the star fruit tree beside his house in the east. He is known as Sonaram master in the village, a teacher with high esteemed personalities: an ideal teacher in deed. He kept his happiness to see his lone daughter, Radha after lapse of one year. He stood up from his work, came near the guests and led them in the sitting room.

Radha went inside a room she used to live her younger days as her personal room. It'd been abandoned after she had passed her matriculation and went to town for her higher education.

"I think you have hard time to visit us?"

"No uncle it has been a pleasant trip," Raj said. "This is the first time for me to visit western part of the district."

"We've enjoyed travelling throughout …" Alice added. "Uncle, it's I who has brought Raj since he was Radha's classmate in the school." Alice liked to be busy in the kitchen she went inside as a helping hand to Radha's mother.

"Nice meeting you, we feel happy when you people visit us," Sonaram complimented.

"Obviously uncle, my daddy, too feel the same," said Raj. "His joy has no bound when he sees his old students visiting him."

"This is the joy for every teacher," Sonaram master said. "We consider it as our pride."

"Yes, uncle … Anyway, Radha was my schoolmate in Golaghat Mission School. She was in the hostel and I was a day scholar. And she was very good in the class."

"Yes, of course, but now she is …!"

Radha brought them tea and snacks. She also sat with them. It was silence for a moment.

"Take tea, no special! Feel yourself homely," Sonaram master had changed his topic to a lighter side.

"It's okay uncle. We, too the same – simple and light every time."

In a little while, Radha's mother came out of her kitchen holding her cup of tea with Alice. They joined with them.

"*Babu*, (a loving common name) take it easy like your own home. We the villagers are like this only. Moreover, your visit is so sudden, we couldn't do any preparation."

"Aunt, we're all same, I'm too, from a village called *Kampur*."

"Oh, I see, your uncle told me about Kampur. He is always proud of Kampur for its uniqueness."

"Uniqueness," Raj said. "What's that ...?"

"I told her, Kampur is the Teacher Factory of Assam. Being a teacher, I'm proud of its sound saying." He delighted.

"It's correct up to this date!" said Raj. "My father, too from Kampur and now he is a retired teacher. And it sounds good to be called a teacher's family, we're proud."

"Well, Babu you talk to your uncle. We'll be in our food factory."

She collected all cups and saucers put them in a tray and entered her kitchen taking Radha and Alice with her. After a bit silence, Raj looked around and outside leaning slightly peeped through the open window closed to his seat.

"Uncle, I'm so sorry to see Radha's condition."

"We do, too! We've tried our best but it hadn't worked."

"Which doctor had treated her?"

"Not Physician Doctor. *Bez*, a kind of village doctor: a witch craft at a far off remote village.

We had kept her under the custody of the *Bez* for more than a month for her treatment before her sudden marriage. But of no use!"

After a pause Sonaram master continued ...

"Some people have told us the same *Bez* had cured their patients, may be we're not lucky enough!"

"This type of witch practice is found every now and then, very strange ...!"

"The village doctor told us it's not a doctor's sickness. He told us it's an evil spirit sent by our aged old family-foe to trouble us." Sonaram master justified.

"Who is the witch and where does he live?"

"His name is *Bonglong*. People don't call him witch, they call him Priest: a Priest Doctor.

He lives at *Longku Sarpo*, a hilly cave locally known as *Longku Sarpo*. He worships Longku – the cave."

"But uncle, actually he is a witch: a practitioner of witchcraft," Raj said.

"Of course, but actually, he is a witch doctor among our tribal people, a magician credited with powers of healing, divination, and protection against the magic of others. Everyone is afraid of him," Sonaram master said.

"Oh! I see …" Raj was thoughtful. "It's nothing sort of that truth."

"But it's an aged old belief a witch-doctor is a type of healer who treats ailments believed to be caused by witchcraft."

"Of course, there was," said Raj. "During those days when all these ailments, and other sicknesses were beyond the reach of an MBBS Doctor or MD, but now …?" Raj gathered the courage to tell Sonaram master the truth about Radha.

"Uncle, in fact, genuinely Radha is suffering from Psychosis," "Her quirks and idiosyncrasies are the results of drug abuse," Raj said convincingly.

"What?"

"Yes uncle, mental disease, and her peculiar habit and behavior are also because of drug."

"What a horrible!"

"Yes, her mental disorder is caused due to consumption of high dose of a certain drug."

"But… how?" He stared at Raj with many questions in his eyes.

"A Psychiatrist, a mental health specialist Doctor can tell it. You better take her to Tezpur Mental Hospital for her treatment. This is the only option," Raj frankly told Sonaram master. He looked down, holding his chin by his hands, confused; couldn't believe his ears!

"Don't worry uncle this isn't the end of her life. We'll help her admitted in a good Rehab Center, nearby," Raj said.

"Thank you," Sonaram said.

"Uncle, this is the reality. Now you've to take Radha for her treatment in this line," Raj benignly pleaded him. Sonaram master plunged into deep thought, he was nervous, and covered with sweat. He was in a fix. Quiescence enraptured the atmosphere it seemed everything hushed in the sitting room.

***

DR. SAM

Dr. Sam was of 1985 batch from a reputed Medical College of Assam. Being a doctor, he'd served the area for more than enough. The last five years service in the remote hilly area among tribal people had multiplied his human attitude of compassion. At quarter to ten, Dr. Sam had finished wearing his gown, the doctor's dress.

"Here's your kit-bag and flask with hot water for you," said Jenny, the doctor's lovely wife.

"Okay darling, thank you," responded Sam with care.

She glanced at Sam, assuring his readiness for the day's duty and hurriedly went in to care her three years old baby. "Okay Jenny, I'm going, take care of Mercy," he gently peeped inside gliding the door's curtain, picked up his black leather kitbag and the flask on his shoulder and set out after simply shutting the door of the house from outside.

After a whole day's hectic duty, attending hundreds of patients, it was time to leave the hospital. A rugged old man came running towards Dr. Sam.

"Sir, please come with me," the old man pleaded.

"Please save my lone daughter, she is dying…" begged with folded palms, tears rolled on his wrinkled cheeks, staring at doctor's eyes for a response.

"Where's your daughter?" looking around and called for a nurse. "Sister, bring the patient in and come with me." Doctor thought the patient might be serious, so he marched on to the Emergency Ward.

"Sir, there's no patient at all!" the nurse reportedly exclaimed. The doctor sharply turned back.

"Where's the patient?" asked the doctor.

"Doctor Sahib, she is at home, crying for immediate treatment," the old man knelt down, crying in front of the doctor….!

"Please save her life," besought the old man again.

The doctor and the nurse looked at each other, thinking what's to be done.

"Sister, ask the man properly in your local dialect," said Doctor

"Tell me in details, I'm here in my chamber," he stayed back.

After sometime, the nurse came in…

"Sir, it's a delivery case," reported the nurse feeling uneasy.

"What!" the doctor wondered!

"Yes sir, it's, the patient is hardly eighteen and she is very critical condition," affirmed the nurse.

The doctor was looking embarrassed, but trying to appease the nervous helpless father.

The village was not near. It was fifteen kilometers away from the hospital. The path leading to the village was not a motorable road, by a motorcycle could reach the village.

By then, the old man was sitting at a corner of the hospital taking the last pub of his local made *bidi*, hoping for the doctor to accompany with him.

The nurse couldn't read the doctor's mind. She puzzled, for he said nothing yet.

"Sir, shall I get ready or …..?" reluctantly asked the nurse.

"No way!" replied the doctor.

"You know, we're in the service of mankind," said the doctor.

"Get ready, let's move," the doctor had taken out the keys of his bike, gave it to his Jeep's driver.

"Robin, here's the key, bring my motorcycle now,""Tell madam that I'm going to see my patient. I'll be late tonight."

Robin hurriedly had taken the keys and went to get the bike for the doctor.

"What to do with the old man?" said the doctor.

"Let him follow us on foot," replied the nurse.

"How comes!" reacted the doctor sharply.

"It's a matter of fifteen kilometers?" worried the doctor. Then, he thought for a while…

"Don't worry, I'll carry two passengers," said the doctor.

"Sir, you mean….?" The nurse said.

"Yes, I mean, I'll carry both of you on my bike," reaffirmed the doctor.

"You know, it's a Jawa Company's *yezdi*," finding no alternative, the doctor proudly acclaimed.

At first, the old man refused to sit on the bike. But the doctor insisted upon him to sit in the middle.

"Don't be afraid, sister will hold you tight," motivated the doctor in a jolly mood.

The doctor had to kick several times to get the bike started. Finally, the bike got started and after he had ensured that they're all set to move, he accelerated his bike for the village, where an innocent soul was fighting with her death. Driver Robin covered his nose with his palm to prevent from inhaling the black smoke came out of the yezdi motorcycle and starred at them amazingly!

It was sad to see the pathetic condition of the father and the daughter. They were poor but pure in hearts. The innocent tribal people were perceptible to everything in every situation. Because, their thoughts were pure and approach were simple and innocence. They knew nothing about the outside world. They had no sense of chaos in the crowded society. They seldom had any idea of cheating others for gain.

The doctor could save the mother but unable to save the baby. For the baby was too immature to be alive. Moreover, the mother was below age and unhealthy, too.

Whatever was the outcome of the situation, the father was happy to see his daughter, *Rani* alive. He burst his tears out of joy and gratitude to the doctor and the nurse. For him, they were more than god and goddess for the moment, for they saved the life of his daughter.

Both the doctor and the nurse enjoyed washing their hands with the pure stream water but without any soap. They took pinch of ashes from the fireplace and used them as an alternative for washing soap. The doctor had taken out his hanky from his pant and wiped his wet hands.

The doctor and the nurse were about to leave the place, when the old man asked them to wait for awhile.

He'd taken out a dried bamboo pipe and from where he hurriedly pulled out pieces of old cloth and took out some paper rolls. Unfolded the paper rolls and few mixed currency notes were taken for giving them as the fee for doctor's visit.

"Sir, I've this amount, saved for my *Rani*," said he with emotion. "Please accept it, sir," he gladly offered the money for keeping his daughter safe and sound. Dr. Sam was at a fix, thinking how to react at the moment. After a pause, he spoke out.

"*Gaonburha*, we respect your concern," coldly uttered the doctor.

"We'll be happy if you offer us a bottle of home-made vodka also," Dr. Sam smilingly asked the man with earnestness. He acted as if the vodka was badly needed for him. The man was for a moment, dramatically convinced and had no option for him but to offer the preserved vodka as demanded. He gladly took out a bottle of vodka from one corner of his thatched and thinly plastered room with mud.

"Sir, this is the one, take it," he offered the vodka along with the few money with his trembling hands. The doctor slowly stretched his right hand and picked up the bottle of vodka leaving the money on the palm of the man.

"Will you mind?" asked Dr. Sam.

For a moment, the old man got nervous; thinking that the money he had offered was too less for the doctor!

"Sir…., your fee…?" he tried to give it again helplessly. Dr. Sam could read his eyes, feel his sense of self-respect. He simply touched the money.

"Keep it with you, it may of your great help in time," he'd looked straight at his eyes and threw his body language - *"Just think that I've given the money for your daughter."*

"Hope, you won't mind now?" smiled the doctor at him.

"No, sir never," replied the man to his heart's content.

"Are you happy now?" Asked the nurse, in order to make him ease and happy. The old man nodded his head.

"Sister, put the bottle in your bag," said the doctor.

Sister was not happy to carry the bottle with her. But to obey her superior, she put it in her bag which made it one kilogram heavier to carry on her shoulder all along the rubbish jerking road.

"Sir, I've never seen you drinking!" asked the nurse slowly in a corner. "Why to-day, sir?" enquired she, again.

"Sister, you won't know it by now," sighed the doctor heavily! "Better you take time to understand..."

"Let's move now, we're already getting late," he tried to divert her mind.

Before they had to depart, the nurse met the patient once again and advised her how to take medicine regularly and care for her health.

"Okay then, *Gaonburha*," Dr. Sam nodded.

"We're taking leave of you." Then both of them stepped towards the motorcycle.

"Thank you for your vodka," said Dr. Sam to acknowledge that they're happy with him.

They said goodbye to the old man, both of them had waved their hands and started back home.

The old man was stunned and surprised at their treatment and compassion! He'd constantly looked at them till they were disappeared in the dark woods, through a zigzag road. He was still holding the money in his hand and couldn't believe himself.

"Amazing, what a surprise, they're my god!" he murmured...!

It was time for breakfast. Generally, Dr. Sam used to prepare some of his favorite menus himself for the breakfast. He enjoyed offering Jenny the early taste of breakfast, almost every morning

Holding one glass of water in each hand, he'd removed the curtain by half of his head and half of his shoulder and peeped in their bedroom.

"If Mercy is not disturbing, come and join with me at the dining table," asked Sam in an inviting mood.

"Here I'm, come on, your breakfast is ready," keeping the glasses of water on the table, he tried to adjust his comfort zone of sitting by stretching his legs upward.

"Lo, I'm on time like every morn," said Jenny charmingly.

"Here's the piece of cake for you, Mrs. Sharma, the compounder's wife had sent it the last evening," she put the cake on the other plate beside. Taking two-three sips of the mushroom soup, Jenny asked Sam.

"By the way, how's your patient last night?"

"She's fine, a bit complicated, but finally cleared up," replied he. "Baby was immature, couldn't save…!" showed sign of discontent.

"Perhaps, Reena sister had accompanied you!" she guessed.

"Yes, obviously, she's hardworking," commented Sam.

At the moment the calling bell was rung.

"Wait, I'll see, you continue," Sam had stood up and went to attend the first guest of the day.

"Oh, you!" "Jenny, here's sister Reena," Sam turned his head back, called Jenny. Reena wanted to wait at the sitting room, almost seated. By the time, Jenny came forth.

"Sister, come on, join with us, we're having our breakfast," Jenny took her at the dining table.

Three of them were delighted to share the morning light meal. Reena felt no uneasiness for she very often had to visit the doctors, by then she seemed to be one of the doctor's family members. Mercy was very fond of sister Reena. She's like family nurse. Moreover, she'd looked after and cared everything for Mercy from the very day of her birth.

"Sir, what had you done with the vodka bottle?" anxiously enquired Reena.

"Vodka bottle!" sprang up Jenny in surprise.

"I'd given it to *Bahadur*, the night guard," replied Sam proudly.

"*Bahadur* was delighted to get the bottle, he looked very happy closing the gate."

Amidst the busy moment of the ongoing breakfast of the doctors, the hardly acquired connected land line telephone rang up…

"Let me attend," said Dr. Sam, hastily reached at the telephone stand and attended the call. Jenny was, as usual anxious to know the call. Dr. Sam kept the receiver and came in again to join them.

"Whose call was that?" asked Jenny anxiously.

"One Mr. Engleng, C n C of an outfit," told he reluctantly.

"Which militant group he's from?"

"Do you think, they do tell such detail?" he clarified her.

"Oh! No, I forgot!" murmured she.

"They'll come to fetch for me, I'm told that the condition of one of them is very critical," Dr. Sam was not in the mood to accompany them.

Police had already given him warning. Many a time, he was called at the Police Station and faced before the Police Officer for interrogations for saving the life of militants. During those days, the so-called big or small groups of militants were strong and actively operating, particularly in the hilly terrains. Many army officers, Police officers and Security Forces were killed in different ambushes. Many encounters between the security forces and the militants had taken place, and countless innocent militant cadres had to lay their lives in vain. Nobody dared stopping the youths from joining in the outfits. The hills experienced the turmoil, the lost of innocent public lives of the hills. The world witnessed the rare massacred, mayhem amongst the hill tribes. The ugliest tortured scene of savages happened so far in the twentieth century of human civilization.

Many doctors, like one Dr. Sam had to face many untoward incidences amidst certain threats and dire consequences for life. They're compelled to maintain a minimum liaison with such banned outfit organizations for their safety and their families. It's the call of the time. No one was escaped or spared.

By the time, Jenny and Reena had had their breakfast and all set to sit a while in the sitting room, while Dr. Sam was ready for another adventure.

It was almost twelve O'clock when Dr. Sam had reached his office chamber. Patients and their guardians were waiting for him to get his treatment. Some patients and guardians had lost their patience for some patients were seriously suffering from malaria, dysentery and typhoid and becoming weaker and weaker. For them, it's almost impossible to wait anymore. Some of them got fainted and created a havoc situation in the hospital.

Out of control, some guardians and attendants got, angry with the doctor scolding him in slant, in un-parliamentary words for his extreme late arrival, delayed attending the patients. It was rush and crowded, for there's no second physician in the hospital. Dr. Sam had adapted with all such familiar situations occurred every now and then in his rural hospital. He'd said nothing but started attending patients one by one in his normal attitude with very calm and cool manner. His surrendering smile and meekness had always won the hearts of many.

That'd been always his great medicine as first aids.

Amid such complex situation, Dr. Sam had to arrange some life saving medicines for the underground patients, who're human, too. He couldn't ignore them at all.

"Sister, call Sharma, the compounder," Dr. Sam asked the attending nurse. Busy writing prescription for the patients, he attended in the morning somewhere in an unknown camp in the jungle.

"Sir, what can I help you?" said Sharma, and waited for the advice. Dr. Sam glanced once and handed over the prescription to him.

"Take this and arrange the medicine," said Dr. Sam gently.

"Sir, some medicines are out of stock, they're to be bought," said Sharma. Sam had taken out some money from his pocket and gave to Sharma.

"I think this will cover up the cost of the medicines," asked the doctor.

"Yes, sir, it'll..." replied Sharma. He had taken the money and went out.

Such and such were the situations, Dr. Sam had to face and adjust with them. He'd taken this as a challenge in life, especially in the life of a doctor. He'd been quite happy serving the poor in his remote village hospital. He enjoyed his works among them and wanted to create memories for life as a doctor.

Resuming his treatment again after a pause, Dr. Sam called his next patient and continued on for the whole day suspending his lunch for the day.

Dr. Sam and Jenny were totally up set. Their only daughter, Mercy was ill for last few days. She was given full medication but her health seemed deteriorating. She couldn't be taken to a better hospital for further treatment. There's a month long closer of the province called by a dreaded militant organization in demand of their statehood. Jenny was totally downhearted. Dr. Sam couldn't understand what wrong with his daughter was. Jenny was trying to bring down the temperature of her daughter by keeping wet cloth on her forehead. She sat worrying.

"What a hell is all this militant! You had helped them in time putting your life in trouble, now this is the result we have to face…" Jenny murmured. Dr. Sam had no answer to this. He kept quiet. In the meantime, the landline telephone rang…

"Go, pick up your phone and go to the jungle and save their lives again. Let your daughter die here…!" Jenny annoyed

Reluctantly Dr. Sam had picked up the receiver….

"We come to know that your daughter is seriously ill?"

"Yes, but who is speaking?"

"Whosoever I'm, forget it. Now listen to me… be ready to go out from the district by tomorrow morning at 4 O'clock. By the time, an Ambulance will be ready at your doorstep."

"But how can we move? Ambush and killing are being taken place in some areas?"

"Leave it to us, have faith on us. Can't we save your daughter's life whereas you've saved hundreds lives of our cadres. We want to see your family smiling. Remember at 4 O'clock sharp in the morning… over."

Dr. Sam couldn't believe his ears. However, he had confidence on them. He knew that they, too human and have hearts. He darted to the bedroom where his daughter was lying on.

"Jenny, get ready, we have to move in early morning… at 4 O'clock. Hurry…!"

"But why, how can we? Don't you know there's a long *Bandh*?"

"Just get ready we can take Mercy out for a better treatment in the city. Arrange things that we need to carry with us." Dr. Sam touched Mercy's forehead. It seemed her temperature had calm down but she didn't open her eyes. He's worried he'd just closed his eyes and prayed.

It was exact 3 O'clock. There're mild knocks at the door. Dr. Sam was already awake. He opened the door and saw an Ambulance standing in front. The driver the Ambulance stood straight.

"Good morning sir, I'm Anthony, the driver…"

Dr. Sam and his family boarded hurriedly in the Ambulance with their minimum luggage, where Reena, the nurse also accompanied with them. On the way to next district, Dr. Sam noticed some escorts with full military uniform at some points at every one kilometer distance. At first, Dr. Sam was afraid but later, he understood it. It's the help from the unknown caller who arranged a Green Corridor for their safe travel. Finally they reached the City Hospital. Dr. Sam and his wife had a sigh of relief.

***

THE BIG DEALS

It was Sunday morning, Mohant, the close accomplice of Vikrant was with Mrs. Ankita at the pergola in front of her mansion. Mrs. Ankita, the wife of Vikrant was worried about her husband. Vikrant was the Chief of a small but very delicate and powerful government in the province of north-east India.

"Madam, you need not worry," Mohant said, "Our Chief is busy with his chief secretary and secretaries in Radison Blu Plaza Hotel in Delhi."

"Why so late this time," Mrs. Ankita said, "It seems he is hiding something from me."

"No, madam, actually it is not of that sort. They are finalizing the Annual Action Plans of all major departments of his government. That's why our Chief is late returning home," Mohant tried to convince her.

"I see, but I am worried, times are not favorable in these days!" Mrs. Ankita said.

The gate keeper, Bahadur had opened the main gate while a newly posted ASI of the local Police Station with his two constables entered and headed towards the Chief's mansion without hesitation but with a smart move.

Mrs. Ankita and Mohant were stunned to see the Police Officer all in a sudden. They were surprised and speechless!

"Don't get panic, I am ASI Bikram from the Police Station to call on the Chief for some urgent legal enquiries," said the officer.

"Well, he is not at home, he is out of station," Mrs. Ankita said, "Please have a seat."

"Thanks, it is okay, where has the Chief gone?" the ASI enquired.

"Our Chief is in Delhi for some official works," Mohant replied.

"Hope, he is coming soon," he said, "Please tell him to meet me in the Police Station as soon as he comes, here is his warrant." The ASI handed it over to Mrs. Ankita and obtained her signature.

The ASI, Bikram and the two constables were off. Mrs. Ankita had seen a Police Officer behaving such a commanding manner for the first time since her husband Vikrant had become the Chief of the Province. Many high ranking Police Officers had come and gone during the last three years of her husband's tenure in the government. They came in humble approach with gift packs and begged her husband for favors. They were sober, gentle and friendly.

"What may be the case that the Police are compelled to issue a warrant to the Chief?" Mrs. Ankita was upset.

"Don't worry madam, I'll meet the Police Officer and enquire the matter," Mohant said.

"Yes, Mohant please," said Mrs. Ankita, "I'm worried about him."

Mohant's heart was trembling inside for he knew the secret of the Chief. His face turned perplexed. He left Mrs. Ankita alone. She had queer thoughts with all pessimistic narratives about her husband.

After three days of the warrant incident. No sooner had the Chief entered his mansion than the famous highest paid

High Court lawyer came in. Mrs. Ankita was in a fix! She couldn't guess anything, so kept on pondering. The lawyer was sitting confidently in the VIP waiting room. After a fifteen-minute wait, the Chief's PA invited the lawyer to the special VIP room: the very confidential room that the Chief had ever made for his discreet activities. The Chief was already inside the room.

"Welcome to my cottage sir," Vikrant greeted the lawyer.

"Thank you sir, it's my pleasure meeting you personally for the first time. Hope everything will be in order," the lawyer said optimistically.

"Hopefully, it will be… if you wish," Vikrant said.

"Well, tell me sir how can I help you?"

"My PA told me that he had already intimated the information pertaining to the case. It's nothing of that sort sir, these are all fabricated and politically motivated," the Chief said.

"Yes sir, but when I have a cross-check of the relevant papers and found it to be a very serious offence: accusation of rap, sexual molestation and harassment as per the FIR lodged against you by one Miss Daisy by name. By the way, do you know her?" the lawyer asked.

"Yah… No, No, I don't know her personally," the Chief replied with a confusing note. The lawyer could collect the first psychological reaction of the Chief. Vikrant was nervous at the sudden question of the lawyer.

"Well, now you have to do some home works."

"What? What do you mean sir?"

"Your highness, relax and cool down."

"Listen to me carefully........., you know my fee is highest among all the High Court advocates," the lawyer betted a bit on the deal.

"Yes sir, I understand. Don't worry about your fee, it's here in this brief case: ten times more than what you have expected and there will added more over the course of time," the Chief smiled at him. The lawyer had shaken hands and took a leave of the Chief. Meanwhile, the PA had already darted the room and picked up the black brief case and kept it inside the INNOVA vehicle. The driver of the advocate took the brief case in his custody with a smart salute.

The very next morning after the visit of the famous lawyer, painters, interior decorators, wall paper designers and electricians gathered together at the Chief's mansion. After they all had their access, the main gate was closed for public entry. Security around the Chief's mansion was beefed up. The public were surprised to see the situation of the in and around of the Chief's personal mansion. On the other hand, the public demanded justice to Miss Daisy and thus intensified the mass agitation for justice.

The living room and the secret VIP room were crowded with electricians, interior decorators, and wall paper fixing experts were busy in their respective professions. The costly fashionable ceiling fans, the costly AC appliances of the rooms were replaced with new make and different brands.

Mrs. Ankita was stunned. She couldn't understand about the urgent need of renovation of her sweet home. Vikrant was restlessly loitering busy in supervising all the ongoing works of renovation of the rooms. Observing the strange behavior and aggressive mood of her husband, somehow she gathered courage to speak to him –

"What's the urgent need of changing all the household appliances even removing my lovely Godrej wardrobe, showcase, bookshelf and the costly furniture of the personal VIP secret room?"

"It's none of your business, mind your own work. It's a matter of prestige and completely political issue," Vikrant said decisively. He was blushed with anger and frustration.

The night was felt the longest of the year for Vikrant. His past mistakes: the crime committed by him had haunted him again and again. He recalled all the lusty magic moments enjoyed with Miss Daisy in the very special VIP secret room as and when Mrs. Ankita was out of station. He was sweating like anything. The illicit affair maintained with Miss Daisy in discreet was a crime. The money power had thrown the Chief into the dark world of sex in multiple in his personal secret life. He pretended to be asleep. But in his heart, fear loomed up. His brain was boiling, his ears became hot unable to sleep. On the other hand Mrs. Ankita was excruciatingly upset and scared. She knew that her husband was not in his sleep. So, in anguish she murmured –

"I don't know what a hell is going on in this home. There's surely nearer to the doom days of the family. I don't know what a sin I have committed! What a hell-life I am living!" Vikrant had heard every word. His heart beats became faster and heavier. Just to give a message that he was in his sound sleep, he snored lightly and took side of his body. But his wife knew it well that Vikrant rarely snored for the last fifteen years of their marriage. So, she started murmuring again.

"Millions of rupees have been wasted in the twinkling of an eye for whose cause? It all had happened only because of your uncounted money and wealth. Having too much money is not a blessing but a curse to the family." The mentally disturbed couple spent a sleepless night.

After a weekend, Miss Daisy was called to the Police Station for interrogation where an FIR was filed against Vikrant accusing him of serious allegation of rape and sexual harassment. Miss Daisy came in her own Mercedes car accompanied by her accomplices. She was tall and bold, a gorgeous girl of her twenties. In her wheat brown complexion, smart looking with straight long and lustrous silky hair. Her complexion was much dazzling in her Ray-Ban sunglass. She looked impressive in her denim blue jean long pant and a jean full shirt of same color matching with her stature. The young ASI, Bikram was stunned looking at Miss Daisy's beauty when she got down from her red Mercedes car followed by her associates.

The attractive girl was sitting in front of the young ASI without any sign of nervousness and fear.

"Yes sir, what can I help you? I'm mentally, spiritually and physically prepared to answer to your queries," Miss Daisy said and eagerly looking at the young officer.

"Do you still claim that whatever allegations leveled against Vikrant, the Chief is true?" the officer asked normally.

"Yes sir, it is hundred percent true," replied Miss Daisy, "Do you think that I can ever afford a Mercedes car without the aid of Vikrant?"

The investigation was quite thorough and prolonged as the Police had to prepare a CD of the case.

The road leading to the mansion of the Chief was deafening due to the noise of cars honking and people shouting. After a long-day restriction by the administration in and around the Chief's mansion the road was crowded again like the release of dam-water. Photographers and reporters jostled for space behind the police barricade, everyone vying for breaking news of the night prime time. It was dusk, the cops blinded by flashlights, were having a tough time managing the crowd. Everyone's eyes were on the Police vans by which Miss Daisy was supposed to bring in the Chief's mansion for showing the spot of the nasty incident of rape in the very personal VIP secret room and the living room where the Chief had called Miss Daisy to quench the thirst of his lust. The DSP and the SP of the province were present at the spot investigation into the alleged sexual harassment case and identification for cross verification with what were recorded in the Police Station as described by Miss Daisy about the in and out of the mansion.

The television channels had already broken the news that Miss Daisy's allegation of rape and sexual harassment against Vikrant: the Chief was proved false and baseless. The descriptions about the furniture, electrical appliances and other descriptions of the living room and the special VIP secret room were all proved false. No evidences as described by Miss Daisy were found but all opposite evidences are available in the rooms. They were not matching at all.

The multitude were astonished and under cold water. Their mouths were dried up. Everything had become up-side-down. The image of the Chief remained unscarred. The public could do nothing except murmuring in their mouths –

"The Chief had bought all: the lawyer and the entire investigating team in term of billion. It's quite injustice, sad… very sad…!" There was hearsay that the Chief had managed Miss Daisy in a deal of crores that made her bound to withdraw the case against the Chief.

After discovering the fact, Mrs. Ankita found the root cause of her husband's fall.

"It was money, the plenty money and property had made Vikrant blind! What a dangerous trend of heinous crime is going on in this world?" Mrs. Ankita was the worst sufferer and the most distressed woman affected due to her husband's case.

"The world is after money, and the money is after wine and women! What a civilized world I'm living in?" Mrs. Ankita regretted with a deep sigh!

***